Pillow Talk

Pillow Talk

A Kane Ridge Ranch Novella

Kane Ridge Ranch

Bailey Johnson

Copyright © 2025 by Bailey Johnson

Cover Design by Megan Parker

All rights reserved.

No part of this book may be reproduced in any form or by any electronic or mechanical means, including information storage and retrieval systems, without written permission from the author, except for the use of brief quotations in a book review.

No part of this book may be used or reproduced in any manner for the purpose of training artificial intelligence technologies or systems.

The characters and events portrayed in this book are fictitious or are used fictitiously. Any similarity to real persons, living or dead, is purely coincidental and not intended by the author.

All brand names and product names used in this book are trademarks, registered trademarks, or trade names of their respective holders. Bailey Johnsons is not associated with any product or vendor in this book.

 Formatted with Vellum

To Ryatt Wilder
and all the babies gone too soon. You are endlessly loved and forever thought about. To the mamas who have empty arms and aching hearts, I see you.

Chapter 1

Chaotic, Messy, Beautiful

Marcy 34

My feet are dragging by the time I make it back to our bedroom. The two youngest boys were a pain to put down tonight. I'm exhausted from running after them all day while also trying to plan for the group of CEO's coming for a retreat next week. Normally I love summer. Having the big kids home from school is my favorite time of year.

This year, though, I feel like I'm drowning. I find myself counting down the days until the end of break. Hating myself for wishing the time away.

"Ready for Delores to be here?" Orson's smooth deep tenor washes over me like a warm hug. I soften at his touch, the corners of my mouth tipping up into a smile when I look into his hazel eyes.

"Yes, does that make me a bad mom?"

"No, it does not." He leans down, whiskers tickling my skin as he presses a kiss to my forehead. "It makes you a mother of six, two of which are still under five, and dare I say, the hardest to manage yet."

"You're right about that." I settle on the edge of the bed, finger combing my hair before taking my socks off.

"Come here love." Orson pulls me up into his arms, carrying me to the bathroom. It's become a bit of a routine for us lately. On the nights when I'm too exhausted to do much more than fall into bed, he carries me to the bathroom where he gets me through my nightly routine before carrying me back to bed.

Never asking for more. Never pressing, just taking care of me in a way I have never experienced before him. My parents were sweet to each other, devoted even, but they were never touchy feely. Not in the way that Orson is. I think I'm partial to his way.

He possesses a tenderness that I don't, one that I hope he's instilling in our boys.

"How were the big boys today?"

"Good," he grins, passing me my toothbrush after squeezing the paste onto it.

"Not too much complaining?" I settle against the mirror, brushing my teeth as he leans his hip into the counter. He's showered, shaved, and brushed his teeth already. The rancher, always ready for bed before the wife somehow.

"Nah, I told 'em we could catch the rodeo in Halstad over the weekend if they worked hard this week."

I raise my eyebrows at him, not at all surprised he did such a thing. Big softy.

"Ethan uh, he had a bit of a melt down though."

"Oh?" I spit into the sink, washing my brush out under the tap, I turn back to my husband.

"Brooks was teasing him, pushed him a little too hard I think."

"Is that what happened to Brooks' face?"

"Hmm," he assents, lifting me from the counter to carry me back to the bedroom. He sets me softly on the mattress, helping remove the rest of my clothing before passing me a nightshirt. When I'm in my pajamas, he shuffles my legs under the covers then tucks me in.

"We missed something this summer," I whisper into the dark when he flicks off the lights. Orson climbs into bed next to me, pulling my body into his massive frame.

At five foot two, I have always felt small, but compared to Orson and now a few of our sons, I feel exponentially smaller. Even my nine year old is taller than I am now. Leni, being the only girl, was supposed to have my stature, but if her growth charts are to be believed, she'll be taller than me soon too.

"I asked him." Orson presses a kiss to my shoulder, snuggling in behind me. "Gave him the chance to talk to me, but he wouldn't. Said there was nothing to share."

"There's something there though, I can feel it. We missed something, Ethan's always been so sweet."

"I know." He sighs, turning onto his back. A faint scratching noise tells me he's twisting his hair together. It's a funny habit he's had since I met him. Sometimes his hair sticks up at odd angles from him twisting it so much. When his beard is long enough, it almost appears to have a cowlick from the repetitive motion.

"He's so angry, have you noticed the way he's started cracking his knuckles?"

"I have." His voice tells me he's smiling, like he thinks this is funny.

"It's not funny. I caught him screaming at Bertie the other day. Poor girl hasn't been back since."

I feel him stiffen beside me, his twisting stopped for the moment. Ethan and Bertie have been best friends since preschool. They argue all the time, but this was different. This was the worst I've ever seen.

"He screamed at her?"

"Yes," I whisper. I don't know what happened to my sweet sensitive little boy this summer, but since turning thirteen, Ethan has been a different kid. "Do we make him talk to someone? Carrying around that kind of anger can't be good for him."

"I don't know, Love, *would* he talk to someone?"

"Probably not," I sigh. These boys and their stubbornness. I'd like to blame him for it, but I know that it's me. The stubbornness, the tempers, all of that comes from me and my side.

"How were the littles today?"

"Ugh," I groan, turning into him as I press freezing cold feet into his calf.

"Jesus Christ woman, give a man some warning next time!" He shudders, but doesn't pull away. Moving his legs to close around my feet, warming me up.

"Leni tried to hex Mercer for eating her cereal again."

A laugh bursts from Orson, the lightness of it contagious as I join him. "Lord help us all."

I snort, snuggling deeper into his chest. "That girl is going to give us a run for our money."

"You said you wanted a girl."

"I did! One that wanted to wear dresses and bows, and paint her nails with me. This is... God, she's got more attitude than the whole state."

"Just how I like 'em." He pecks me on the temple. A chuckle rumbling through his chest.

"Fuck off," I grumble.

"And the boys?" he prompts, turning onto his side so that I can see his eyes glimmer in the dim lighting.

"Adler damn near bit through his tongue today, he didn't cry. Toby did, when he noticed all the blood. I called the ER and they said there was nothing they could do. So he's walking around with a hole in his tongue for now. I think we're going to have to take him in."

A heavy weight fills my chest at the thought of subjecting my perfect two-year-old to the whims of doctors and specialists. Biologically, everything seems to be okay. All of the blood tests we've run so far come back completely normal, but Adler never cries. At least not in pain. He's racked his head, fallen off counters, been run over by the older boys and still, he doesn't cry. Today when he opened his mouth to empty it of the blood, I thought for sure he'd start screaming, even with a flap of his tongue hanging off, he didn't so much as whimper.

"I'm scared," I whisper into the dark. Orson pulls me to him, wrapping an arm around me, the other tucking under my neck.

"Me too," he breathes. "We'll figure it out, love. Your mom will come help with the littles, the older kids will all start school soon, and after these next two retreats, you can focus on Adler."

"What if we can't fix it?"

"He doesn't need fixed, Love. He just needs us. Once we know how to help him, how to keep him safe, he'll be fine."

"You promise?"

"I promise."

"Do you think that's what's bothering Ethan? He dropped that stupid horse statue on Addy's foot the other day. His face went white as a sheet, but Addy just stared at him. Maybe he's worried too?"

"Could be, I think they're all starting to notice that something is different."

"If I wasn't so busy, if I had just prioritized him a little more, then maybe we'd know what happened, maybe we could find a way to fix it."

"Marcy Jo, why do you think it's your sole responsibility to fix everything?"

"They're my kids." I sit up on an elbow, looking down at him. "It is my job—"

"Our," he interrupts me.

"*Our* job to protect them, to guide them. We missed something and that's our fault."

"We might have missed something, or maybe it's just puberty. He's thirteen, things happen. Maybe him and Bertie fighting is where it's coming from. Maybe there's a girl that broke his heart. There could be a million different things, but until he's ready to share it, all we can do is be there for him. Support him, love him. Even if he is a crabby little asshole lately."

I huff a laugh, collapsing back onto my side next to him.

"Speaking of girls." I turn back towards him. "I've noticed a black haired beauty wandering around by the barn a time or two. I don't recognize her from town."

"Ahh, yes, Kate. She's taking riding lessons from Brooks."

The way Orson says, *riding lessons*, lets me know that that is not at all what she's here for.

"Is she new to Hillcreek?"

"Mhm, moved here last year with her dad. Brooks talked about her a time or two before school let out for summer. Just yesterday he was asking me how to ask a girl out on a date."

"Orson!" I groan. "You didn't tell me that!"

"It was confidential." I can hear the smile in his voice. "Brooks specifically said, 'don't tell Ma.'"

"That means you're obligated to tell me, asshole."

He chuckles, deep and light. "Is that so, Love?"

"Yes, that's so."

"Hmm." His fingers pull me back into him. Exploring

lower on my thighs, trailing little pinpricks of fire down my skin as he goes. "I'll tell you anything you want to know."

His whisper is dark as sin, stoking that fire low in my belly. Fifteen years with this man and he still turns my insides to mush when he talks to me like that.

I used to worry I'd resent him. Told him I wouldn't marry him when I turned eighteen and he proposed. He was only nineteen at the time, we were both babies, and I was convinced I had to see what else was out there. He gave me the space I asked for, but never let me forget he existed. Never let me forget what I was missing. Six months later we were married, and nine months after that we brought our first born, Brooks Elliott Kane into the world.

Ranching was hard to get used to, having a baby on top of it meant we spent very little time together those first couple years. My mom came and stayed a few times, told me it would be worth it, if I stuck it out. Guess she was right, I can't imagine a life without my best friend, without our six unruly children constantly running laps around us. It might not be perfect, but it is bliss.

Chaotic, messy, beautiful bliss.

"Have I told you lately, how much I fucking love you?" I frame his face in both my hands, pulling him closer yet.

"You know, I don't think you have, Love."

"I really." I pull at his lips with my own. "Fucking." I kiss him again, dropping one hand from his face to trail it down his chest. "Love you," I breathe into him. Kissing him hard, as my hand snakes below the waistband of his briefs.

He groans into my mouth, flipping me onto my back as he rears over me. I slip his briefs down his legs, widening my own so he can fit his hips to mine.

"I really fucking love you too," he whispers back. "Happy birthday, Love."

I live for these little stolen moments. When there's quiet and I get him all to myself. There's no ranch talk, no kids, just me and Orson. And nothing else matters.

Moments like these let my mind shut off, all the guilt and worry melting away with every heated touch. Every gentle reminder that I am loved wholly and completely for exactly who I am in this moment.

Chapter 2

Wild and Headstrong

Orson 38

"MARCE, YOU IN HERE?" I CALL INTO OUR BEDROOM, wondering where in the hell my wife has gotten to.

"In here," she calls from the direction of the bathroom. I shed my clothes on the way there, about to join her in a bath, or find my way to the shower. I won't lie, I'm hoping it's the bath, today was a hard day. Rain pelted us as we moved the herd out of the sevens. While it's been a warm summer, today's high was seventy, the real feel coming in at around sixty seven with the wind and the rain.

The boys were in good spirits, despite the weather, but I am feeling the strain on my muscles.

To my relief, Marcy is half buried under bubbles in our jacuzzi tub. Her eyes rake over my body. Taking in the muscles and scars, appreciation shimmering in her eyes.

"Why Orson Kane, you look as good as the day I met you."

My chest fills with warmth, emotion clogging my throat as I take her in. I knew the second I laid eyes on

Marcy, when she was sixteen, that I was going to marry her. Once she walked into that classroom, there was no one else for me. No one else in the entire world would do.

It had to be her.

Still does, if I'm honest. Her dark hair is still long and thick, thick enough to need two braids when she winds it back. There are a few wrinkles in the corners of her eyes, a little frown line in between her eyebrows. Her skin still tans in the summers, freckles playing out across the tops of her cheeks and nose, just like Leni's.

Marcy's green eyes soften when mine meet them. I didn't realize how easy it would be to completely lose myself in her. I don't know who I am without her, and I am one hundred percent okay with that.

"You coming in Mr. Kane?" Her voice skates over me, sending goosebumps all over my body.

"Just enjoying the view." I wink, hooking a leg over the edge of the tub before I sink down into scalding hot water. I hiss a breath out, wide eyes looking up into a maniacal smile on Marcy's face.

"Why does it have to be the temperature of lava? Are you trying to burn our skin off?"

"This has cooled off since I got in," she croons at me, wading across the tub until she settles between my legs. "Thought you'd like a nice hot bath after being out in that rain all day."

"Hot, yes," I grunt, sliding down further so I can rest my head on the lip of the tub. Pulling Marcy further into my lap. "This is boiling us alive."

She grins at me, that feral glint in her eyes that used to always be there. I never felt like I lost the girl I fell in love with, but there have been many versions of her over the years. I've loved every single one of those versions. Even when that little spark is missing.

Leaning her head back into my shoulder, Marcy sighs. Running her hands through the water in front of us. Her body settling deeper into mine. I've nearly dosed off when she starts up the conversation again.

"Leni's smitten with Mercer's new friend." Marcy moves to the side so she can grin up at me, watching my reaction.

"Saw that too huh?" I sigh, blowing out a sharp breath.

"He's a sweet kid, she could have picked someone much worse for a first crush."

I chuckle. She's not wrong. Clayton Traeger might have been born to a shitty home life, but he's a good kid. One that's been just as good for Mercer as Mercer has been for him.

"They don't seem to mind her tagging along for everything either," she muses, running her hands through the bubbles in front of her.

"Are you kidding? Mercer wouldn't know what to do without his little shadow. I don't know how he's going to ever leave here if Leni can't go with him."

She laughs, the sweet melodic sound echoing around the room like a song. "They're so close, I'm glad they have each other. I was worried, with the bigger age gap."

Her gaze goes out the window, shoulders tensing a little at the reminder. There's a tree out back where we buried not one, but three little ones who didn't make it home to us. Two were early losses, Marcy had barely known she was pregnant with those two. The other was at twenty weeks. Between Leni and Toby. A little girl we called Winnie.

Those losses sit between us, sacred scars on our souls that tether us together even more. The years haven't made it easier, thinking about what could have been. What should have been. Nothing can bring those babies back to us, but I make sure she knows that I see her. That I recognize the pain in her, twin to my own.

Every due date, I buy her flowers, and on the date she birthed our second girl, I make sure she has whatever she needs.

Sometimes it's a private birthday party, just the two of us and the baby girl we never got to meet. Sometimes it's a day out, other times it's as simple as making sure the kids are taken care of so she can retreat into herself.

Whatever the need is, I try to make sure it's met. Somehow she pushed through all of that pain and sorrow, and gave me two more beautiful children. I wouldn't have blamed her for stopping after that loss, wouldn't have blamed her for giving up after any of them.

Not my Marcy though. Not my strong, beautiful, determined wife.

Lifting my hand from the water, I grip the back of her neck, tilting it back so that I can press a kiss to her lips. Her mouth curves up in a smile before she opens to me. Her body melts into mine like it belongs there. Because it does.

She is mine, and I am irrevocably hers.

When my hands have pruned and the water is damn near chilled, I reluctantly climb out of the tub and head for bed. Watching Marcy as she moves, her body still as graceful at thirty-seven as it was at twenty-two. I could sit and watch her all day, if there wasn't so much work for both of us to do.

"So, how was the drive then? How'd the boys do in the rain?"

"They loved it," I chuckle. "You should've seen the three of 'em before I hosed them off at the barn. They were covered in mud."

"Sounds about right." She shakes her head, settling onto the mattress.

"How'd you make out with the littles then?" I tuck her into bed before turning out the light, sliding in on my side until our bodies are flush together. My hands seeking her out, tucking her in closer.

"Don't let Leni catch you calling her a little, Pa."

I snort into her hair, tucking a wild strand back behind her ear before I nuzzle into her neck. "She's still little though, right? I haven't completely lost my little girl?"

"You? Never. It's me I'm worried about. We keep butting heads, it's like she does the opposite of what I say just to see what happens."

"Ethan went through the same thing, remember? She'll come out of it."

"God I hope so, raising girls was supposed to be cute. The boys are so much easier."

"Even the littles?"

She sighs, long and heavy. "Okay, maybe it's a toss up. Toby told me I didn't need to check Adler for new injuries tonight, because he did it."

Her voice grows heavy with emotion. The sound of a thick swallow sitting in the space between us.

"I didn't want this for either of them, they're kids. They shouldn't have to worry about this."

"I know," I murmur, pressing a kiss to her forehead. "I know, Love."

My own throat grows thick with emotion. This is not what I wanted for my boys either. Adler was diagnosed with Congenital Insensitivity to Pain. He can't feel it when he gets hurt, a condition that is terrifying when you're raising a toddler who is constantly running into things and lives on a ranch.

"I've never been scared to live on this ranch with you, but when I see him watch you guys, the way that yearning grows in his eyes." She shakes her head into my shoulder. "They both feel it, the way they aren't included. Leni was in a saddle for years at this age. Are we doing the right thing?"

"I don't know, I don't know how to keep him safe."

"There has to be a balance, he has to be able to be a kid, but still be safe, right?"

"Bubble wrap?" I choke out, trying to hold back a laugh. She barks a laugh for me, turning around so that she's facing me.

"Got any horses broke enough to carry around a bubble baby?"

"Should have, somewhere," I grin into the dark like an idiot.

"Kate was around again today," she grumbles at me. The smile falling right off my face. I forgot, somehow, that Brooks mentioned proposing. I don't know how to tell Marcy that her eldest is looking to hitch his wagon to a girl she's come to despise.

I'm not sure when it happened, but suddenly the two of them were at odds. Poor Brooks dumped right into the middle of their feud. Kate might not be as bad as Marcy makes her out to be, but I can't stand the idea of anyone making my wife uncomfortable in her own house. Around her own family.

"About Kate..." I steel my resolve, trying to prepare for whatever reaction she might have.

"Don't you dare," she groans, turning onto her back, her hands coming up to her face. "Please don't fucking say it, I can't take it."

"He thinks they're us," I whisper, trying to soften the blow.

"They are not us," Marcy spits. "She will never be a Kane,

she will never be good enough. She's two-faced and downright malicious."

"He doesn't see it yet."

"Well hopefully he does, before she does something unforgivable and breaks his heart beyond repair."

"He's talking about proposing."

Marcy's hands shake above her chest, like she's imagining shaking some sense into Brooks.

"Why, why are they all so damn stubborn? Not a single one of them knows what's good for themselves yet, and they all insist on giving me grey hairs."

"He'll figure it out, they all will."

"What?" She turns to me, her eyes glistening in the moonlight that's creeping through the windows.

"That you're always right, of course."

She laughs and I know if I could see her better, she'd be smiling ear to ear. The same smile that knocks the breath out of me every time I see it. She's so goddamn beautiful.

"Well they better learn it soon, I'm tired of saying I told you so."

"Better get used to it Marcy Jo, these kids are every bit as wild and headstrong as you were growing up."

"Don't I know it. That's what I'm afraid of."

"They're good kids." I stroke a finger down her cheek, tucking more waves behind her ear. "We're doing alright by them, I promise."

"God I hope so," she whispers into my chest.

"Ethan still talking about law school?"

"Mhm," she breathes into me, her body sinking deeper into the pillow top mattress below us. "Eight years," she whispers, her voice cracking. "He's going to end up on the other side of the country and how do I take care of him there? How do I make sure he's eating? Drinking enough water?"

"You do all that for the next two years, Love. Teach him how to take care of himself. He'll find his way back."

"What if he doesn't? What if he really does decide to go to law school and he likes the big city life? What if this town isn't enough for him?"

"It ended up being enough for you." I remind her gently. There was a time when Marcy swore she'd leave the first chance she got. That middle of nowhere Halfor County would never be enough for her.

Now, when we do manage to sneak off for a family vacation, she hates leaving more than I do. She's always the first of us ready to come back home. Her and Brooks acting like they're going through withdrawals the longer they're away from Kane land.

"This place is in his blood, he'll come back."

"This better be one of those times you get to say I told you so, because I don't know how to live across the country from one of my kids. I wasn't built for that."

"I know, Love." I tuck her in a little deeper. Drawing her lips into a kiss that tells her I know. I know her fears and her faults, and I will hold her through each one. There is no better mother for this crazy brood we have. Even with the anxiety and the guilt, she's the only one for this job.

"At least Brooks isn't going anywhere."

"Ugh. Marce, you're always killing the moment."

She giggles, a sound that doesn't come out often. One I've learned to cherish.

"Sorry, I just—when did they get so grown? How is it that we have children talking about marriage and college and rodeo?"

I shudder at that last one. For the past several years the boys have competed in team roping events, Ethan and Brooks even trying their hand at bull dogging. Mercer, now, can't shake the idea of bronc riding. I'm not sure my heart can take that kind of trauma. Watching my son get flung around on the back of some animal intent on killing him.

It's hard enough watching the two older ones train the colts.

"Let's try to discourage that for a few more years."

"I already told Marty Tyson that none of my boys are to get on a bronc unless they're legal adults."

"Thank God you're scary when you wanna be, I'm not ready for that yet."

"Don't think you're getting him out of the steer wrestling though."

"I know." I sigh, resting my chin on her head. "Suppose we win some and lose some hey?"

"Mhm," she mumbles. Her fingers tracing lazy circles on my skin as we drift off to sleep.

Chapter 3

Hey Mama

Marcy 38

"How is he?" Orson sets his book on the side table when I finally make my way into our room. He leans back against the headboard, that big muscular body of his stretched out across the mattress. He's showered and ready for bed, only this time he kept the beard. Just like I asked. I like the hint of gray he's getting. The way it's peppered through his dark facial hair.

"Okay, I think. He's settled in with Mercer for the night." I sit on the edge of the bed next to him, running my fingers through that beard. Enjoying the weight of him as he leans his face into my palm.

"Did you tell him there's a spare room for him?" Orson kisses the heel of my hand before reaching back to let my hair down. Raking his fingers through from my scalp to the ends. I moan at the quiet comfort in the action. "Of course, he didn't want to be alone."

"Understandable." His hands move down to my neck, massaging my tight muscles.

"How did it go with Caleb? Do you think there will be any trouble?"

"Nah." Strong fingers dig into my shoulder blades, more indecent moans slipping from my lips. "We had a little heart to heart, he won't come looking for him."

"We'll need something giving us legal rights, for school and doctors—"

"Took care of that too. Ethan printed something off for me, told me what steps to take."

"So we're still on the lawyer track, huh?"

"Oh definitely." Orson pulls me up between his legs, settling his arms around my waist. His chin drops down to rest on my shoulder as he breathes me in.

"Looks like you got there at the right time." I tip my head to the side, turning to look up at him.

Clay called the house phone just before dinner, screaming for help. I've never seen my son so scared. Orson grabbed Brooks and headed straight into town. Mercer stayed on the line with Clay, until Caleb took the phone.

"I know we joke about the temper's being from your side, but I've never felt a rage like I did today. He had him pinned to the floor when we got there, beating the shit out of him. I don't know what might have happened if we hadn't shown up."

My heart sinks at the thought of it. What drove a parent to hurting their own child like that? How long had Clay been fending for himself, hiding the bruises from us?

I've never seen a child so badly injured, and I'm raising five boys on a ranch. Clay's left eye was swollen shut by the time they got back, his lip split open, and his two front teeth chipped. His cheek was bruising as well, and I saw the handprint on his neck. Like Caleb had grabbed him by the throat and squeezed.

I reach for my own throat, sorrow welling deep within me.

"I pulled him off Clay and focused on getting him up. Making sure nothing was broken. Pretty sure he has a few cracked ribs, but fuck..." Orson shudders behind me, that rage building back up as he relives the memory. "By the time I turned around, Brooks had laid Caleb out flat. I had to wait for him to come to before we could talk."

"Jesus." I run a shaky hand through my hair, leaning my head back into his chest. No matter how many times I find myself here, I can't seem to stop myself from memorizing every little thing about him. The way he smells like horses and lemons. The way his chest feels behind me, rising and falling in time to my own.

There's a thin scar that runs down his left arm, that one an accident with the barbed wire. A thicker white scar on his right thumb from some mechanical issue or other. I think I could map his whole body from memory. Every single little thing that makes him Orson, makes him mine.

"Should we get him into therapy?" I half joke, knowing Clay is every bit as stubborn as our own kids.

"Let's just let him settle in a little, yeah? Let him start the healing process."

I sigh, pressing a kiss to Orson's cheek. "What's one more boy, eh?"

"Exactly," he chuckles behind me. "He knows the rules about Leni?"

"He does, Brooks and Ethan made sure he knew the rules about Leni's room, just like they do everyone else who stays over."

"Think we're hypocritical with her?"

"How?"

"Well, we've got no rules about Bertie staying with Ethan."

I pause for a second, momentarily surprised. "Ethan and Bertie are worse than siblings, I really doubt we have to worry about them."

He chuckles into my ear as I snuggle in deeper, drawing my knees up into my chest. "How long was Clay living like that? How did we not see how bad it was?"

"I think it's been like that his whole life," he sighs into my hair. "I think he's gotten so used to hiding it, or people not taking it seriously, that it was just normal for him."

"I wish we would have seen how bad it was sooner, wish we could have done more for him."

"Oh Marcy." He hugs me even tighter. "Not every wrong in the world can be fixed by you, Love. Not every hurt is your responsibility. Clay might not have known love before, but he will now. You can be the Ma he's always needed, and that is enough. You are enough, my love."

Tears fill my eyes as I think of all the things I've missed while running my business. My mom has basically taken over full care of the younger boys, the older ones all busy with school, or in Brooks' case, working the ranch.

I feel like there's never enough of me to go around, like I'm always missing some little detail that has overarching consequences I can't see until it's too late.

I knew living on this ranch wouldn't be easy. I knew being a mom would be hard, but it was supposed to get easier, wasn't it? When does it actually get easier?

"Adler's started pretending to be in pain."

"What?" Orson huffs a soft laugh, his body relaxing deeper into the bed. One sure sign he's working his way toward sleep.

"Him and Toby have worked out a system, if something should hurt, Toby gives him some kind of signal and Adler starts howling like he's in pain. It's unsettling as fuck."

Orson barks out a laugh, one that's part shock and part amusement. It's funny, kind of. Mostly, I think it's sad. I caught Adler fake a cry the other day, his eyes shooting up to Brooks, checking to make sure he was right. Like he was looking for approval from his big brother, and I think my heart nearly shattered.

"That's certainly one way to go about it." I can feel Orson shake his head behind me. "What else have they been up to?"

"They're building a fort somewhere in the trees after school. Mom has been supervising."

"Now that's terrifying," he chuckles.

It's true. My mother with any kind of tool in her hands is a scary prospect. We once had to hire a professional contractor to fix the structural damage she created when she tried to renovate her room here. Turns out, load bearing doesn't really mean much to a woman in her seventies with an idea in her brain.

"At least the fort isn't part of some larger structure." I can't keep from grinning.

"God save the trees," he laughs behind me. "Leni and Miya have fun overnight camping?"

"No." I burst into laughter. The image of our eleven year old coming back home in the middle of the night with her best friend, covered in mud, looking pissed as hell sends me into hysterics. "Oh God, they were a mess. I tried, Lord, I tried not to laugh but the look on her face when she had to concede."

"She does not like to lose," he muses.

"No she does not." I shake off the laughter, rolling out of his lap, onto my back so I can look up at him. "Good thing you didn't bring Clay home last night, imagine the horror."

"I thought for sure she'd move past this little crush by now." Orson strokes his chin, running fingers through his facial hair.

"I'm not sure she's ever moving past this crush."

He groans, slipping down the headboard until he's laying

flat on his back too. "She's supposed to think boys are gross and stay with me forever."

"Sorry hon, she's growing up."

"They all are, Brooks showed me something gold and shiny today."

"Ugh," I groan into my pillow, trying to let the disappointment go. I've been trying, I swear I have, but I cannot get myself to like this girl. Things have gotten better between us since she moved in. Her mom left with a boyfriend and Kate's been here on the ranch ever since.

Brooks asked me to give her a job with my retreat company, so I did. I have zero complaints for her as an employee, yet...I can't shake the fact that she still doesn't deserve my son. I don't like her well enough to welcome her into the family, but how do you tell your first born son that you hate his girl? That you can't stand the thought of her being here for the rest of your life. The idea of her inheriting anything on this land makes me sick to my stomach.

"I thought things were getting better." Orson tucks hair back behind my ear, his fingers trailing down my shoulders until he's rubbing small circles on my arm.

"I don't hate her, I just...hate her for our son."

"A noble distinction."

I toss my hand back, smacking his bicep. "She's not right for our family, and you know it."

"For the family, or you, Love?"

Pushing up onto my elbows, I turn to glare at my husband. He's being intentionally obtuse. Kate is a nice enough girl, but she is not the future wife of our son. I might not pull the mom card about everything, but I have a gut feeling that sours every time I try to picture a future with her around. She isn't a good fit.

"Fine," Orson concedes. "She's not the one, but she's the

one right now and we need to let our children make their own choices."

"Well I hate that," I grumble, lowering my upper body back down onto the bed. "I know better," I groan into the mattress, my voice muffled.

"Mhm." Orson pats my head like I'm a child.

"What if they get married before he realizes how wrong she is for him?" I roll over to look at him, feeling petulant.

"Then he'll have to pay for a divorce." He shrugs.

"What if she tried to take the house? Take the land?"

That gets his hackles up. He might be the laid back to my high strung, but Orson cares deeply about this land. He offered to portion out spots for the kids, under the single condition that they sell it back to a sibling if they ever consider leaving. He will not see Kane land go to an outsider.

"There's gonna have to be a prenup." He looks at me, eyes dead serious.

"Now we're talking." I sit up, grinning like a mad woman. "Think Brooks will go for it?"

"He's gonna have to." Orson sits up too, his eyes as bright and fierce as mine right now. Oh, yes, Mr. Kane is fully on board. I love it when he gets all riled up and takes my side.

"Well, before he pops the question, I think we should talk to him about it."

"I agree." He barely gets the words out before I tackle him backward onto the bed.

My lips crash into his, taking his mouth in a scorching kiss. Big calloused hands slide up the sides of my body, hauling me, up and over him. One swing of his leg and I'm rolled beneath him, safe and sound and cozy underneath this perfect man of mine.

"Hey Mama," he murmurs into my neck. Pressing kisses down my jaw.

"Hello Mr. Kane." I smile into his shoulder, my teeth nipping through his t-shirt.

He brings his face back over mine, looking down at me. The look of concentration on his face says his thoughts are not heading in the same direction as mine.

"What's she like?" He cocks his head to the side, leaning down on an elbow. "What's the future Mrs. Brooks Kane like in your head?"

"Now who's the mood killer?" I furrow my brow at him, no doubt reinforcing the frown lines I have forming.

"Indulge me, I'll make it worth your while." The grin he gives me makes me shiver. He certainly will, I've no doubt about that.

I take a moment to think, picturing the woman that would make an acceptable partner for my son. I don't care what she looks like, just as long as she's the opposite of Kate, personality wise.

"She's bright and sunny. Maybe a little quirky? She can't be serious, at least not too serious. Brooks needs someone that's fun, someone that reminds him to *be* fun. Most importantly, though, she loves him. Not for what he can give her, not for the house he can build her, but for him. The man who cares too much, the man who breaks his back to give her everything she deserves."

"Yeah," Orson breathes, dropping his forehead onto my temple. "That sounds about right for him."

"Told you, I know best."

"Hey, I never doubted that." He winks at me, coming back onto his knees so he can work my shirt over my head. "Now about that promise..." His voice drops low and sensual.

I hum into him, the feeling of his fingers on my skin setting me on fire.

Worth my while indeed.

Chapter 4

I Am Nothing Without You

Marcy 40

My body feels leaden, my limbs heavier than tree trunks. I'm barely sitting upright, and yet, I can't let my eyes close. When my eyes close, my heart breaks and I can't breathe.

I stare across the apartment, my eyes barely able to focus on the tiny form in the bed there. They had to sedate him, and now my nine year old is sleeping off a medication that was only necessary because I couldn't calm him.

Tears streak down my cheeks, I can feel them, but I can't bring myself to wipe them away. The utter exhaustion, the pure agony of being here alone numbs any part of me that might have cared.

There's a knock on the door, but I don't answer. I can't stop seeing Adler with skin dripping off his hand. Can't stop picturing the fear in his eyes as they hooked him up to tubes and put him under anesthesia.

"He might not feel the pain, but that doesn't mean his body won't go into shock from the trauma." Some random doctor spouted random shit I didn't hear as they wheeled my baby away. He's staying in the burn unit, being kept under sedation for the night. All alone.

A sob racks my body. I feel like it's being pulled from the depths of my soul, shredding me from the inside out. I'm fucking drowning.

Toby stirs in the bed, so I muffle my sobs in my shirt. Trying not to wake him. He's been through so much already.

A knock sounds again, and this time, I hear Orson's voice muffled through the wood.

I rush through the door, slamming into him with so much force, he's knocked back into the hallway. I lose it completely, burrowing into him as I let myself fall apart.

I don't know how long we stay in the hallway, my body shaking as he holds me on the ground, keeping me tightly wrapped inside his arms. Grounding me.

I'm all but passed out when he tips my chin up, searching my eyes for anymore signs of tears.

"What happened?" His voice is raw—thick and full of emotion. I know, somewhere in the back of my brain that he's asking for a run down of the incident, not blaming me. And yet, my hackles raise and I feel the rage bubbling inside of me.

"I told you," I hiss. Pushing off his chest to stand. "I told you we shouldn't go without you. You promised, you said that we would be fine."

"So it's my fault then?" Orson stands, towering over me by over a foot. "Who was watching him,?"

"I can't be everywhere at once!"

"You had seven teenagers with you and not a single one could have helped watch the littles?"

"I was tending to Leni's bee sting, the older kids were putting the tents up, he—"

"Shouldn't have been left unsupervised by a fucking campfire." A rare glint of fury slices through his gaze.

Suddenly the weight of it all crashes down on me and I can't breathe. More tears spill from my eyes, and I hate myself. I hate that I didn't make sure someone was watching him. I hate that Toby had to push his little brother out of a fire. Hate that he had to ride, terrified, in a helicopter because he wouldn't be separated from me. I hate that they had to sedate him because he wouldn't stop screaming. I hate that my youngest is currently tucked away in a sterile hospital bed by himself while my older children are all dispersed between friends, away from us. Above all, I hate that I'm the reason it happened. I hate that I stepped away.

I hate it.

Hate me.

"I know," I whimer, more tears flooding my cheeks. "I should've...I—" words are too hard right now. My whole body heaving, trying to get air into lungs that refuse to make room. A broken cry bursts out of me and he's there in a second. Wrapping me up so completely my feet aren't even on the ground anymore.

"No, Love." His voice is firm, the kind of voice he reserves for ranch hands or crooked dealerships. Not the kind, gentle voice he uses on us. "I'm scared, but this is not your fault. I should have been there. I'm so fucking sorry I wasn't there."

Orson's voice cracks, his shoulders shaking on a sob and I'm so broken I can't even comfort him. I don't know how to move past this, how to continue living our lives like this never happened. Like everything is normal when our eight year old is so desperate to be like everyone else that he would do something like this.

"How is he?" Orson's voice comes out hoarse and I know he's holding back more tears.

"They're keeping him sedated tonight, he's... he's all alone in there. They wouldn't let me stay, especially not with Toby here too."

I use my sleeve to wipe my face, then tip my hand up to wipe his too.

"And Toby?"

"They had to sedate him too," I whisper. "Less aggressively, they gave him some kind of liquid medicine to calm him down. He's sleeping it off in there. He was hysterical, I couldn't calm him down. Couldn't be there for Adler the way that he needed because I was dealing with Toby."

Shame pushes in on me, the weight of it stooping my shoulders, stealing my oxygen.

"Fuck." He sets me down on my feet again, propping me up against the wall, because it's too much to stand alone right now. "I should have been there, I should have been here."

His head hangs down, dark brown waves toppling forward. This is one of the rare times I've seen him out of the house without a hat on. It's either in the truck, or blew off when he galloped back to the big barn. However he lost it, it's a sign of just how desperate the situation is.

"Leni didn't want to leave the hospital." My voice shakes, her pleas echoing through my head on a loop. "She didn't want to be alone without us."

"I got a call from Iva on the way in." He smooths a loose strand of hair away from my face. "The boys snuck in."

"What?" I choke out what might be half sob half laugh.

"I don't know if she called them, or if they just needed their girl, but Iva caught them climbing up a ladder into Miya's room."

"All of them?"

"All of them, Brooks too. I don't know what Bert and Kate

saw, but it doesn't seem to have shaken them as much as the boys."

"I tried not to let any of them see it. Mercer puked, Ethan looked like he was going to pass out, and surprisingly, the one who kept his head was Clay. He helped me get Addy wrapped up before anyone else saw it, and I think that probably made it worse."

"Are there concerns for infection?"

"Yes." My head tips back, Orson's hand catching it just before it connects with the concrete wall behind me. His fingers knead into my skull, some of the tension fizzling out. "Toby tackled him into the dirt, and then I went and wrapped it up, and fuck. It's too much Orson, this is too much."

I dig my hands into my eyes, hoping that maybe, if I can just push hard enough, all of this will go away.

"It is," he murmurs, his head dropping down to rest on my shoulder.

We must look ridiculous, standing around in the hallway of the hospital family wing. Trying to piece ourselves together.

"Your mom and Iva are planning on driving the kids up tomorrow, Leland left as soon as I called, he should be getting to the ranch with Hawken by now. Him and Keith can keep things going until we figure things out here."

"Are you sure?"

"I'm positive. I should have come on the trip, I should have been there for you, I'm not leaving you again. Not leaving our boys again."

"Okay." Fresh tears slip down my cheeks. I have no idea how there's anymore left in me. I couldn't tell you the last time I ate or drank anything.

"Ma!" A heart shattering cry comes from the little apartment we're staying at in the hospital. It's a studio apartment, more like a hotel room, but it's a miracle they had one open. I told them we would be sleeping in the waiting room if we had to, but I wasn't leaving my baby in this building by himself.

"Ma!" Toby's sobbing intensifies, calling back the way he nearly passed out from crying so hard earlier. Orson takes my hand and leads me into the apartment.

"We're here, Bud," he murmurs into the dimly lit room. Toby launches himself off the bed, flying into Orson's arms the second he's close enough.

He's blubbering, incoherently, clinging to Orson so tight his knuckles turn white. I rub his back, humming his favorite lullaby as he cries himself back to sleep. When I look up at Orson, his face is streaked with new tears, his arms shaking from how much he's having to hold himself back.

"Come on," I whisper, tugging him back toward the bed. He lays Toby between us, one big arm draped over him so that he can put his hand in mine.

I curl around our son, pressing a kiss to his head before I look to Orson.

"I'm not good at this," I admit. "I don't...I don't remember it being this hard when the older ones were little."

"It was hard," he murmurs. "But it was a different kind of hard."

I nod, thinking back to the times when I felt utterly wrecked by motherhood. Being a young mom was hard, and now, being an 'old' mom feels even harder.

"The shitty parts of me wonders if I pushed my luck," I drop my eyes down to Toby's hair. It's lighter than the rest of ours, soft and fine, instead of coarse and thick like everyone else's. I let him keep it longer, because I'm a little bit obsessed with it myself.

"What do you mean?"

"What if this is punishment? What if we were meant to stop having kids after we lost Winnie and this is payback for pushing my luck? For wanting more when we already had so much?"

"Oh, Love." His hand tightens around mine, and I know, if we didn't have Toby between us, he would be crushing me into him. I can't stop the next round of tears from falling. "You are not being punished, it's not a crime to want more, to want more than the futures we lost. You are an incredible mother, and all of us are lucky to have you."

"Then why? Why is this so hard? I know. I know how blessed we are, I know that we're lucky, but this is too much. This is too hard."

I expect a pep talk, expect him to tell me that we can do hard things. That there's nothing we can't get through together, only he doesn't say that at all. He doesn't pressure me into finding the bright side, doesn't tell me that I have to push through. Instead, he laces his fingers through mine, and squeezes my hand.

"So let it be what it is. For tonight, for however long you need, let it be too hard. I don't know what the future holds, I don't know when it will feel more manageable, when life will ease up. But this is hard. It's too hard, too much. There's no point in trying to change that, no bandaid is going to fix this."

More tears rush down my face, I almost think I'd prefer if he told me to buck up. Feeling this depth of emotion is torture, it's all consuming. I have known darkness during years of post-partum depression, I've known pain and sorrow after our losses, but this? Admitting that I'm not enough, that this is too much, is breaking me apart.

I asked for this life, I wanted these boys, and yet, I'm barely keeping it together, on a good day.

"I want to take a break." The words taste bitter in my mouth. Failure cutting deep into my marrow. His hand tightens in mine, fear or disappointment maybe, making him cling to me.

"A break?"

I turn my gaze up to him, searching his eyes and I can see the panic there. "I thought—" I stop myself from speaking. Dread coiling in my gut. "Ori, I thought the ranch was doing okay, I thought—"

"The ranch? Fuck the ranch, if you think you need a break, I don't...fuck." He tries to pull his hand away, his muscles quivering from something I'm not understanding.

"Just for a little while," I plead. "I'll finish out the retreats already booked out for the rest of the year, but then I just want some time. I need to remember what's important, figure out who I am in this season of life."

Sorrow fills his eyes as he takes me in. I didn't expect him to take this so hard, didn't think he would be anything but supportive. If the ranch was doing well, it shouldn't matter if I stop hosting retreats for a while.

"I am nothing without you," he whispers, his voice watery. "Tell me what to do, Love. I'd sell the whole fucking thing if you asked me to."

"What?" I screech, causing Toby to flinch between us. "What the fuck are you talking about Orson? You can't sell the ranch."

"I can and I will, I am not going to lose you. If you think for one second that I would choose that place over you..." He blows out a breath, his fingers twitching in my hand, itching to run through his hair, or twist it.

"Orson," I hiss, my eyes wide, my whole body shaking as I try not to laugh. Hysteria bubbling up in my throat. "I don't want a break from you, you stupid, stupid man. I want a break from work. I don't want to schedule any new retreats."

He stares at me, blinking for several seconds before his shoulders drop down from his ears, his eyes shuttering closed.

"Fucking hell, woman." Glassy hazel irises look back at me when he opens his eyelids. "I thought you were trying to leave me."

"You're an idiot." I can't stop the maniacal laughter that rips out of me. "I'm nothing without you. God, I don't even know how to pump my own gas, could you imagine? The last thing I will ever want a break from is you, Lover."

"Thank fuck." He turns onto his back, pressing his free hand to his chest. His heart's probably pounding so hard it hurts. "There's a lot of things that I can push my way through, Marcy, but life without you ain't one of them."

"I feel the same about you."

Pulling my hand over Toby, he presses his lips to my skin, then turns his head to look at me.

"I mean it. You ever need to leave this place behind, you say the word. The ranch means nothing to me if I can't have you."

"I love the ranch, I love our life. I love raising our babies at the main house. I just need to get out, breathe some fresh air. Focus on our kids, on us."

"Do it." H squeezes his fingers still wrapped around mine. "Take as much time as you need. Hell, if I never have to see another city slicker in alligator boots again, I'd die a happy man."

I smack his forearm, then bring his hand up to my lips. "Forever isn't long enough, Orson, but I'll keep you all the same."

Chapter 5

We Don't Fight Like That

Orson 42

"Holy shit!" I scoop Marcy off the floor, swinging her around in circles before I topple us onto the bed. Dizzy and maybe a little tipsy. Mostly, high on life though. "Did you see that shit?"

"Yes Ori," she laughs, playfully hitting my chest as she sits up on an elbow. "I thought we agreed not to encourage this."

"I know," I groan, threading my fingers through my hair as I look toward the ceiling. "That was an incredible ride."

I'm no better than a fan girl, my eyes full of stars for my eighteen year old son. Mercer made his first bareback bronc ride tonight and it was a thing of beauty. He took home the buckle on his first ride, like he was born to fucking do it.

I haven't stopped smiling since he jumped off that bucking horse and threw his hat up into the air. I've no doubt he's getting into plenty of trouble with the girls who were lined up waiting to talk to him after that spectacle.

"He did well." Marcy's smile dims. She hated every single

one of those eight seconds. My right hand ended up with little half moon indentations from where her nails dug into my skin. Her grip punishing for the whole ride.

"They're old broncs." I try to make it seem a little better. A little safer. Truth is, I was terrified too, but watching that kid of ours crush it? Watching the sheer joy on his face when he beamed up at us? How could I not be infected by this joyous all consuming pride?

"Don't belittle my fears. He could have fucking died, and you know it as well as I do. Your own Pa ended up crippled being thrown from a horse, and that one was trained to ride."

"I know." I sigh. Feeling my shoulders deflate. I never was one for rodeo, too busy working the ranch, learning how to take it over. My best friend Leland was a rodeo champ, he rode professionally until his wife passed and he ended up a single dad of two. His oldest boy has already started high school rodeo, and I wouldn't be surprised if one or both of them end up going pro.

"It really was incredible, wasn't it? The way he moved with that horse." Marcy's voice changes, a little bit of awe coming through. I glance at her, the shimmer in her eyes all I need to let that joy inflate again.

Reaching up I tuck silver streaked hair behind her ear. The gray has been coming in for both of us lately. Neither one of us caring enough to take the time to get it covered. Personally, I think she looks just as beautiful, if not more, as the day I met her.

"Did you see that line of girls rush him when he walked around the stands?"

"Yes, I saw them, the whole county saw them." She's shaking her head, but her smile is back in full force. Tonight was a good night. For all of us. All of us but Brooks.

"I can't believe Brooks missed it."

Marcy's face darkens, unadulterated rage taking hold. "I told you." She narrows her eyes at me, one finger jabbing into my chest.

"I never argued it." I glare right back at her. Fully knowing it will only serve to aggravate her more. Aggravated Marcy is one of my favorites.

"When is he going to say enough is enough? Is it not bad enough that she cheated on him? Now he's spending his nights bailing her out of jail, trying to get her sober enough to have half a conversation?"

She's fuming, pacing back and forth at the end of the bed while I watch her.

"Marce, we agreed, he has to make his own decisions. He'll resent us more if we try to force it."

"She's killing him." Marcy turns to me, the passion in her voice hitting me square in the chest. I sit up in the bed, planting my feet on the ground. I pull her hips forward, tugging her into me. "There's no joy in his eyes anymore. He works so hard and for what? For her to go out drinking? Partying?"

"He will figure it out, the boys give him hell for it. Shit, if anything, Leni and the littles will do it."

"Oh?" Marcy quirks an eyebrow at me, her fingers reaching back to play with the hair at the nape of my neck.

"I overheard him with Leni yesterday, she walked right up to him and asked if he was mad at her."

Marcy's eyes widen, her mouth opening and closing, once, then twice. Trying to decide if she wants to let me finish or not. The look on poor Brooks' face was pure agony. He's been pulling away from the family for some time now. Pouring all his energy into paying off his house, and caring for Kate when she's hungover or wasted. It's not the life I wanted for him, that's for sure.

"He asked her why she'd think that, and she said it was

because he never smiled at her anymore. And he missed family dinner, so she wanted to make sure she didn't do anything to upset him."

"Ugh, shot him right in the chest did she?"

"She did," I chuckle, tucking more hair behind Marcy's ears.

"That girl worries too much about everyone else around her. She'd run herself ragged trying to fix everything if we let her." Marcy drops her hands to her sides with a sigh.

"Huh." I quirk an eyebrow at her. "Doesn't sound like anyone I know."

"Oh shut up you." She whacks me on the shoulder before moving toward her dresser. Taking off her fancy jewelry that she saves for special occasions. Like our middle born son riding his first ever bronc.

"The littles were pretty jazzed up tonight." I kick off my boots and hang my belt up in the closet. Moving to the buttons on my dress shirt. Marcy wasn't the only one who cleaned up well for tonight. The whole family was looking mighty fine.

"They hate that we call them that," she grins at me, a glint in her eyes when I remove the shirt and put it up on the hanger it came off earlier.

"Well someone needs to be a little." I sigh. "They're all growing too damn fast."

"They are," she groans. "You think Ethan will keep track of Mercer and Clay tonight? I know the fair is safe, but I also know the boys are going to drink."

"Not Clay," I muse. Clay will barely touch alcohol. Only occasionally drinking a beer here or there, and even then, I usually catch him dumping some out by the end of the night. "He'll take care of them—him and Bertie."

"Bertie is also dating an asshole." Marcy puts a hand on her hip. "What is it with these kids choosing the worst possible partners?"

I snort, "Now you know who's right for Bertie?"

"Of course I do." Marcy widens her stance, gearing up for battle.

"Fine then, describe Bertie's perfect match."

"Easy," she scoffs, "Ethan."

I choke on my own saliva, pounding on my chest as I try to work it down the wrong tube. "Ethan?"

"Mhm." she joins me by the bed, rubbing circles on my back as I continue to hack.

"Ethan and Bertie? Are you crazy? Those two fight like cats and dogs."

"Like an old married couple, you mean." She winks at me, letting the tie at the end of her braid go, she finger combs her hair. The soft scent of vanilla wafting into my nose.

"We're an old married couple and we don't fight like that."

"That's because..." Marcy swings a leg over my lap, settling her hands on my shoulders before sinking down onto my thighs. "We have a different form of foreplay."

"Jesus," I whisper, about to point out that nothing romantic has happened between Ethan and Bert, and maybe we shouldn't refer to our children and foreplay in the same sentence...but her mouth comes crashing down onto mine. Any thoughts or objections I had in me all but lost on a breeze.

Breaking our kiss I haul her into me, lifting her up so I can lay her out on the bed beneath me. "God damn I'm a lucky man."

After a quick shower, we've got our teeth brushed and the lights turned off. Marcy tucked in beside me in the bed.

"So, how much did they bet on each other?"

I can't hold back my grin, knowing exactly who she's referring to. Toby and Adler have taken to placing bets on every little thing. What started as a funny joke between the two of them has turned into a full fledged gambling ring amongst all the siblings. There's a bet for almost everything nowadays.

"Three months of no stall mucking goes to the winner."

Marcy chuckles, nuzzling herself even closer into my side. "They fail to realize they won't actually be mucking stalls when they're eighteen huh?"

"Never know, it depends on who they piss off that day."

"True." I rub the back of her neck, earning me a little sigh. "Who won the bet for Mercer's ride?"

I groan at the thought of Adler's smug swagger tonight. That little cheat came out almost two hundred dollars richer. Not that we all didn't believe in Mercer, I just never guessed he'd do that well. Somehow, the nine year old knew he'd get the buckle. Swore it up and down, believing in his big brother so much that he bet two months worth of cookies against some pretty serious cash from the older kids.

"Does that mean I have to make him more cookies?"

"Hell no, he made out well enough without any added sugar."

"He's smart," she muses. "Like, really smart. Ethan might have the book smarts, but Adler is something else."

"He is." I sigh. The kid's a hustler, he knows how to work a room to get what he wants, and I don't know if that's just compensation for his disability, or what. "How did he do with the trial?"

Marcy and the three younger kids spent a good portion of their summer staying in another state. Adler undergoing a clinical trial to help study and understand CIP better. Toby and

Leni begged for the change of scenery, so off they went with Delores. It looked like they had a blast.

Ever since Adler's extended hospital stay, I've been trying to encourage Marcy to take the time she needs. We haven't done any more corporate retreats, and it's been a healthy change for her.

We're working out a plan for when she gets back to it, but I think I'll have some stipulations of my own. For starters, staff. We can afford it, so she needs to hire it. I won't have her coming so close to burnout that she's questioning her worth with this family. Never again.

"He did well, though he kindly asks to never do one again. Said he missed the ranch too much, complained he's already behind on his horsemanship."

"I don't know, we put those two on horses later than the others, and I don't think that I've seen better riders. They're naturals."

"Oh I know." Her jaw cracks on a yawn. "We went out to the swimming hole yesterday, neither one used a saddle, and you'd think those horses were just an extension of them."

"How are *you* feeling after the trial?"

"Better." She props herself up on an elbow, moonlight reflecting back at me from her eyes. "It helped meeting people who are also dealing with it. Meeting adults who gave me hope, and fellow parents who know what we're going through. Who can relate."

"Good, I'm glad you were all able to go. How was Leni in a big city?"

"Different," she muses. "She seemed to come alive there, like she was unfurling her wings. I'm worried we're going to lose her when she's grown."

"She'd come back, if she leaves."

"I admire your confidence." She sighs.

"Ethan's already talking about coming back, Love. He's only two years in and he's already making plans for when he gets back. Just, don't lose hope if she does leave, yeah? Everyone needs to spread their wings a little."

"I suppose."

"Speaking of, spreading wings..."

"I swear to God, Orson, if you tell me Mercer changed to an East Coast school I might scream."

"No, Mercer's still attending Benson Community College, it's Clay."

"Clay?" She stares down at me, some of that hurt I felt earlier when he talked to me echoed in her eyes.

Clay took to ranching like a pig takes to mud. You'd have thought he was born here, the way he works the land. The kid is a natural with horses and I've never seen a better roper, for a kid who's only been doing it for three years.

I honestly thought he'd stick around, pick a little spot on the ranch and live here with the rest of us.

"He enlisted." The words taste a lot like disappointment in my mouth. Clay isn't ours, but he might as well be. I'm proud of him, proud of the man he's become in just the few short years he's been here with us. Hell, I'm even proud that he wants to go off and protect our country, but I'm fucking hurt too. Hurt he didn't tell us, hurt he planned to leave, and well, maybe even a little disappointed he didn't want to stay.

"Enlisted? With who? Why? When?"

"Guess a recruiter for the Marines came by the school in the spring. He was already eighteen, so he joined. Kept it a secret so he didn't hurt any feelings, but he leaves next week."

"Next week?" Marcy lays back down, her fingers pressing into her temples. "I don't understand."

"Me either. I wish...I don't know what I wish for. I might

have tried to talk him out of it, might have told him not to go, so I guess it's better I don't wish."

"You wanted him to stay, to help Brooks when he takes over the ranch."

"Yeah," I whisper. Secretly hoping Clay didn't feel any of that disappointment when he talked to me about it. He has enough self-doubt as it is, I don't need to be adding anything to it.

"Well, if you're right, then he'll come back. Just like you claim the rest of them will."

"God I hope so, I've become kind of fond of the little shit."

"He's one of ours." Soft lips press to my cheek before she pulls away. "He's gonna get an earful from me tomorrow, keeping a secret like that until the last minute. If he thinks he's getting away without some kind of shindig to send him off he's got another thing coming."

"You know Clay doesn't like to make a fuss. Let him say goodbye in the way that feels right to him."

I can practically feel her brows furrow at me. "And what if that way was writing a note and leaving without so much as a goodbye? Because the week before really isn't that much better."

"He still doesn't believe we're here for him long term. His own mother left him, let him figure it out however he needs to."

"You know? You tell me what to do a lot, for someone who insists other people need to be left to make their own decisions."

A laugh bursts from my chest, shaking the whole bed frame beneath us. "Last I checked, you didn't mind it so much when I told you what to do."

She hums into me, soft, cherry flavored lips pulling at mine until she sinks back into the bed.

"So I don't."

Chapter 6

Stubborn and Foul Mouthed

Marcy 42

I'm tucked into the bed, my hair braided back, book in hand by the time Orson makes his way into the room. He stops to peck the top of my head before heading to the bathroom, the sound of the shower starting echoes through the room.

I settle back into the romance novel I started yesterday. I'm only halfway through and I have to say, these characters are spicy. I've taken to hiding my books in here, anywhere else in the house is apparently fair game. Lord knows I do not need my ten and eleven year old sons reading them. It was bad enough finding Mercer reading one the other day.

He claimed that the textbooks in school were rotting his brain and he needed some good cliterature. I about fell out of my chair when he said it. His face completely straight, not a hint that he was joking until he saw the way I reacted to it. The little shit.

It's nice having him back home for summers. I've missed

him, missed all my boys. Clay writes us letters when he can, mostly, though, he writes Leni. I'm not sure when that started, but every week we go to check the mail, and there's a letter in his blocky handwriting with her name on it.

Orson comes back into the bedroom, a spicy woodsy scent coming off of him in waves. He falls onto the bed with a groan, the towel still wrapped around his waist.

"I'm ready to retire," he mumbles into the mattress. I snort, this man is not going to retire, he's going to work this land until his last breath.

"That bad huh?"

"Just a shit show with the colts today. Two of the hands ended up in the ER and Brooks had to leave early. Again."

"Kate?" I ask.

"Mm." Orson tips onto his side, one eyebrow quirking at the photo on the cover of my book. There's a cowboy with long flowing hair, no shirt, brand new work gloves and a rope that looks like it's fresh from the store on the cover. He might not be a real cowboy, but he sure is nice to look at.

"I'm done with her," I say, thoughts wandering to the hell Kate's put my son through.

"I think Brooks might be done with her too."

"Finally." I sigh, tucking my book mark between the pages, I close the paperback and set it on my nightstand. "How many times has he taken her back now?"

"Too many to count, he's loyal to a fault."

"Hmm." I lean forward, slipping my hands through his waves, more and more gray peaking through every day now. "Speaking of loyal, Leni got another letter today."

"Another one huh? Have we gotten to read any of these letters?"

"No, she keeps them pretty close to the vest. It pisses Mercer off to no end. Guess he was getting more letters at college, but since summer started, Leni's the one getting them."

"I'd like to know what they talk about..." He rolls over, heading for the dresser to grab a pair of briefs before climbing under the covers with me.

"I trust Clay." I shuffle closer, seeking the warmth from his skin.

"Fuck your toes are cold," he groans, tucking my feet between his legs to warm them up. "I trust Clay, but she's in love with him."

"Pretty sure he's in love with her too."

Orson groans into me, hiding his face on my shoulder.

"She's only fifteen, she's not supposed to be in love yet."

"If I recall correctly, I was sixteen when I met you." I poke his cheek, a smile playing on my lips when he turns to look one eye up at me.

"Exactly, sixteen. She's too young."

I chuckle, shaking my head.

"Let me guess, you think Clay is the perfect match for her then, do you?"

"I don't know, I go back and forth on that."

"Really?" He sits up on his elbow now, head tilted to the side as he considers me.

"She's stubborn and foul-mouthed, I don't think Clay minds those qualities, but she's too much of a people pleaser. Always putting herself last, and Clay, he's terrified he's not enough. Right now, I think it's best if they just stay friends. Leni needs to figure out who she is before she breaks herself open trying to take care of other people."

"Stubborn and foul mouthed you say? Couldn't be my Leni girl."

I smile down at him. "I made a joke one time about her

being more lady like and I swear, she took that as a challenge to be as foul as possible."

"That girl is worse than a sailor, she made Leland's oldest blush the other day."

"Oh my God, she's out of control." I can't stop the little burst of pride for my girl though. We might butt heads here and here but she is every bit the woman I hoped she would be. "The Fisher's had a quick trip this time."

"Yeah." Orson turns onto his back, his fingers twisting in his damp hair. "Ransom's going for his pro card this year."

"Already? He's still underage."

"He'll be eighteen middle of the season, sounds like they're making an exception for him. He's good." Orson turns to smile at me. "Real good, better than Leland I'd say."

"Well then, I hope he does well. He'll make his dad proud."

"Oh for sure. You ready to watch Mercer ride more broncs this year?"

"No, yes? God, I've come to love it. I'm so proud of him, but also, thank God he's not trying to do it for a living."

"It's a different kind of life, for sure. I can't wait for him to get back home full time. I miss my boy. Both of them, all three of them, really."

I see the sorrow in his eyes. Him and Brooks used to be thick as thieves. Ever since Brooks moved out and in with Kate, he's become distant to all of us. The littles feel it, but none more than Orson I think. He's hurting for our son, and he doesn't know how to help him. Neither of us do.

Ethan's back home for the summer as well, working the ranch instead of hanging out with his friends this year. Bertie's boyfriend doesn't like how close they are, he actually tried to chase Ethan off a time or two. He's not that easy to scare off though, none of our kids are.

"Why haven't you asked about Mercer?" I change the

subject, avoiding the heavier conversation we could be having tonight.

"What do you mean?"

"About his perfect person, you haven't asked who I see for him."

"Ah, that's because I know the perfect person for Mercer." Orson grins at me, a playful glint in his eye. I raise a brow at him, prompting him to elaborate. "Mercer needs someone strong—no nonsense. He needs someone to bring a little more seriousness into his life. But she has to be willing to try new things, willing to laugh at his jokes. Someone who can handle his special brand of drama."

"You mean not the buckle bunnies who follow him around the fair?"

"No, definitely not them," he chuckles. "Mercer needs someone who will appreciate how big his love is."

"He's a romantic, remember when Heidi Smith told him he was too much?"

"Yes." Orson perks up, a dopey kind of grin spreading across his face. "What was it he said to her?"

"If you want less, just say so." I drop my voice lower to mimic Mercer's. Heidi called him clingy and too much. Mercer shook her off like a bad joke and kept going. At least one of my kids knows his worth.

Orson barks out a laugh, his head falling back into the mattress as he howls. "Oh she was pissed, remember the way she stormed out of here?"

"I remember." I shake my head. "That girl was trouble with a capital T. I'm glad Merc didn't waste more time with her."

"Have you liked *any* of the people our kids have dated?"

"I mean..." I try to think about it. I haven't known any of the girls Ethan has dated, he never brought one home in high school, and with him going to school so far away, I doubt I'll meet one anytime soon. Brooks fell for Kate and hasn't been with anyone else since. Mercer only dated Heidi for a couple of months, before they fizzled out. Him and Clay always seemed too busy to date, so no. I don't think I have.

"If they'd just consult me before dating, it would sure save everyone a load of trouble."

Orson grins at me, reaching up to boop my nose before he settles deeper into the mattress, crossing his hands over his chest. "How's Delores?"

I lay on my side, tucking one hand under my pillow. "Not well," I whisper.

We had to make the difficult decision to put my mother in a nursing home three months ago. Her memory has been fading more and more. Hard as it was keeping tabs on her, I wish we had never put her in that place. The decline was almost immediate. The strong, effervescent woman that raised me was nowhere in sight.

"She was doing fine here, I shouldn't have pushed for the home. I should have kept her here, hired a nurse or... I don't know. That place is killing her Orson."

Shame fills me up, making it hard to look at him.

"If you think that's what's for the best, then bring her back." He says this with an even voice, one that holds no judgement, or criticism. I peek an eye open at him, taking in his relaxed stance, the way he almost looks like he's sleeping.

"What's the catch?"

"No catch." He shrugs.

"Then I want to move her back."

"Good." He shrugs again, my temper sparking to life because I know him, I know he has something else to say. "Then you're sure it's for the best for your mom to be back here."

"Yes, of course, I'm sure."

"And you're sure that it's in your best interests too? To have her here. To constantly be worried she didn't slip her nurse and is wandering the grounds. You won't be up all night, sitting in her room, making sure she stays in bed?"

"I..." Will absolutely be doing all of those things. But that's not fair, she's my mother, and he knows it. I'm about to tell him off when he steamrolls me.

"You're absolutely positive that it's for the best for our children to watch your mother slip away slowly, turning into a version of herself that doesn't remember them or the time they've spent with her? You're sure that bringing her back here is for the best of every one involved?"

I groan, yanking the pillow out from under my head I slam it onto his.

"Fuck you and your logic," I furrow my brows at him, but there's no venom in my words. I'm not mad, because the truth is, I need him to tell me that this is okay. That I'm not the world's worst daughter. That having her there is actually the best. I need him to absolve this guilt that I'm feeling, and that's exactly why he's doing this.

"Marcy." He gets up onto his knees, crawling towards me. "Delores was starting to decline here, not just her memories, but her body too. It might feel sped up now, but you don't see her every day anymore either."

I sit up, objections on my tongue when he puts a finger to my lips.

"I am not blaming you, nor am I trying to shame you. I do not envy the balance you have been forced to keep every single day. You are doing the best for your mom. Getting her the care and safety she needs, while also protecting our children as they process losing someone who helped shape them. Someone who is still here, but somehow already gone."

The softness in his voice nearly shatters me. How is it that he always knows exactly what I need to hear? Exactly when I need to hear it?

I look up at him through my lashes, my breath catching at the fire his eyes hold in them. The way he's staring down at me.

"I am in constant awe of you, my love." Warm calloused fingers reach back to wrap around my neck, drawing me up as he comes down to meet me.

His lips catch mine, soft yet firm at the same time. His gentle kisses turning into something more, something hungry.

In all the time that I've known him, Orson has been cool, calm, and collected. He's the level headed, always patient, ever kind soul that quiets me in a way no one else could.

The respect I have for him is unmatched and I love every single thing about him. But the thing I love the most, is the way he unravels for me. The way all of that composure disintegrates the moment we're behind closed doors.

Out there, he is this imposing, immovable force that I know, without a shadow of a doubt, will always be there to pick me up when I falter.

But in here

In this sacred space that is just ours, I get to watch him lose control.

For me.

Over me.

Twenty-five years of being his and it never ceases to amaze me just how right he is for me.

Chapter 7

For Better or Worse

Orson 46

I WAIT IN THE HALLWAY LIKE A COWARD. LISTENING through the walls to hear the shower start up.

Once it does, I sneak into the bedroom, slipping into a pair of sweatpants. I hate this, the fighting—the avoiding. It's unnatural, but I don't know how to find my way back to her. Not this time.

The moment my hand reaches for my pillow, I hear the floorboards outside the bathroom creak.

"Orson, I swear to God, if you take that pillow and sleep on the couch one more time..." Her voice waivers, choked with emotions too big for me to handle tonight.

I stare at the cotton pillow case, my heart begging me to go to her. To forgive her and move forward. I flex my fingers, curling them into a fist, before I slip under the covers.

I don't hear her walk away, but the shower turns off, the bed dipping when she climbs into it. I keep my back to her, like a child, hugging my arms around my middle to keep myself from reaching for her.

The silence is deafening, weighing me down like a physical force. We've argued, sure, but I've never spent this long being mad at her. Never spent a single night out on that couch until last week, when she told our eighteen year old daughter not to come back.

I've excused her temper before, given her a pass for the words she spoke out of anger, but that...How does she ever come back from that? How do we move forward after that?

Sheets rustle and I can picture her curling in on herself. Her tiny frame, looking more like a ball in the massive bed, tucked up into one small fraction of it. It isn't long before the mattress starts to shake, her silent sobs wracking through her body.

It's another reason I moved myself out to the couch. There is no instance where I can sit here and listen to my wife sob without doing something to comfort her. As mad as I'd like to stay at her, I wasn't made to endure this.

I last all of ten seconds before I turn to her. A gut wrenching cry escapes her as I pull her into my arms. I hold her while she weeps, big messy tears that soak through my shirt. My own tracking down my cheeks, slipping over my nose and into my ears.

What a fucking mess we've made.

Time is irrelevant in a moment like this. It doesn't stand still, I know, but it doesn't move forward like normal either. It falters, stuck in a moment of absolute broken surrender.

We lay in silence once her tears have dried up. I listen to her shallow breaths, the kind that shakes on the exhale, gasping air in on the inhale.

"I can—" she whispers into the dark, her voice raw, aching. "I can live with me hating myself. I can, I'm used to it, but you..." She hiccups another sob, my arms instinctively gripping her tighter to me. "I can't live with you hating me."

"I don't," I murmur into her hair. It doesn't sound convincing, but it's the truth. I don't hate her, but I can't condone her actions either. Not when we both know that something happened this past year when Leni went to find Clay. She came back different, came back hurting and we pushed her away. Backed her into a corner until she broke and didn't feel safe enough to come to us. "I just, I need to understand. How could you?"

"I didn't mean it," she cries. "I didn't, fuck, I didn't mean it. I wasn't even thinking it, it just came out. She's so goddamn stubborn, she needs us. She needs—"

"Help," I say quietly. "She needed help, Marcy. Not ultimatums, not threats. She needed us—you, unconditionally in her corner and you..." I can't finish the words, my voice shaking as anger and sorrow swirl in my gut, burrowing deep into my bones.

"I felt like we were losing her, I-I hate myself."

I can't find the words to tell her she shouldn't, that everything will be okay. Truth is, I wouldn't blame Leni if she never came back. And it's that thought that kept me on that couch for the past seven nights.

There's this hollowness inside of me that I just don't know how to fill right now.

"I've tried calling." Marcy's chest is still heaving, more sobs ebbing just under the surface, waiting to burst out of her. "She won't answer."

I nod, words still eluding me. Marcy and I have always been a team, no matter the argument, no matter the issue. We have always been a united front where the kids were concerned, working our disagreements out behind closed doors.

"I know I fucked up, I know I lost her. I know that."

"What do you want from me? Do you want me to tell you that it's okay? That we'll find a way past this?"

Her body stiffens in my arms, her chest inflating as she takes a breath. Holding it there.

"It's not okay. We are not okay. I don't..." I let go with one arm, letting my fingers run over my head, more skin than hair on top now. "If she never—" My voice breaks. "I can't choose between you."

"I know. I wouldn't ask you to, not after the way I behaved. Not after what I said. She needs someone, even the boys—"

"Took your lead," I mumble. A stone dropping into my stomach as I recall the harsh words spoken to Leni by her brothers. And I didn't call them on it, not a single one of them. I let her leave with her eyes full of tears. Her hands stuffed full of cash from my safe, like that somehow made it better.

"I'm going to make it right." A determined edge sets in her voice. I know she'll try, but I don't know if there is a way to make this right. "I have to."

"How can I help?"

"Just tell me she's okay."

I sigh, recalling the short text message Leni sent me when she made it to Benson. She wouldn't tell me where she was staying, if she found temporary lodging to keep her safe before the semester starts.

"She's as okay as she can be. She's strong, though, like her Ma."

"God," Marcy scoffs. "I hope she's not like me."

I chuckle, my arms softening around her, my body melting into hers like it's coming home for the first time in months.

"She is all the best parts of you, Love."

"And you," she whispers, her head tipping to the side so she can press her lips to my arm. "I've missed you."

"I've missed you too." I let her in closer, let the anger fade out as my heart lifts for the first time in days.

"I've missed our pillow talk." I know she's trying to lighten the mood, move on from the heavier topics into safer territory. I let her, welcoming the chance to let the hurt go. Even if it's just for this moment.

"Was I seeing things, or did Toby have a black eye?"

"Oh, it's definitely a black eye."

"What happened there?"

"Do you want the story he's telling people, or the one I saw with my own two eyes?"

"Both." Her voice rushes out. Grasping at the sense of normalcy in the conversation.

"Toby's version involves a poorly placed elbow during a wrestling match. What I saw was our abnormally tall fourteen year old cornering Hawken Fisher in the barn."

"They were fighting? The boys never fight with the Fishers."

"Not exactly," I chuckle, the memory still fresh in my brain. "Toby kissed him."

Marcy squeals, unable to keep herself from turning around to face me. "He kissed him?"

"He did." I shake my head. "Hawken punched him, then apologized profusely. I'm not sure who was more embarrassed in the end."

"God, I missed it. Toby's first kiss." She lays back down, her fingers twining in my t-shirt, keeping me close. "Is that who you see for him? Someone like Hawken Fisher?"

"God, no. At least, I hope not. Kenny's a cocky little asshole."

That makes her laugh and God, that sound is sweet. It washes over the fraying edges of my heart, soothing them.

"I can't really see Toby with any one person, can you?"

"No, not really," she admits. "I've tried to see it, multiple times. I think I just need him to grow up a little more, figure out who he is. Then I'll see it."

"Maybe," I offer, my hand idly rubbing up and down her arm. "How's Mercer settling back in?"

"Good, I think. He seems to be doing well, how is he at work?"

"Fine. He's always been a hard worker, always keeps himself busy. Brooks gets halfway to telling someone where to go, and Mercer's already there, doing whatever it is that needs doing."

"Are you still thinking about cutting back hours? Giving Brooks a little more control?"

"I'm not sure more work is what Brooks needs at the moment."

Brooks finally broke ties with Kate for good, only, he's still distant. He comes to work, and goes straight home. I don't think he ever goes out with the boys, and if he does, he doesn't stay out long. He's overworked and under cared for.

"He didn't just lose Kate," she whispers. "He lost a whole future. We know what that feels like."

It's a low blow, and she knows it. Wednesday was the first time I missed Winnie's birthday. The first time in sixteen years that I let her think it slipped my mind. It didn't. With everything happening with Leni, Winnie has been heavy on my heart.

I sat under her tree, watching the barn for hours. Wondering what she would have been like. What she'd be feeling right now, having watched the way her Ma treated her big sister. How things would be different, that maybe none of this would have happened if she was still here. If we hadn't lost her.

"I saw your flowers." Marcy looks up at me, her eyes glassy

again. "I know you didn't forget. I just wish you would have spent some time with me."

My sigh is heavy, loaded with all the words we haven't said. All the words we won't because neither one of us wants to punish the other any more.

"I get it." Hurt laces her normally sweet cadence. Her muscles locking up as she moves to slide away from me. Back to the other side of the bed.

"Don't." I grip her waist, moving myself into her. Holding her to me in the middle of the bed. "Now that I'm here, I'm not letting you go. I'm still mad, I still don't know how we work through this, how we fix it. But you're mine. For better or worse, Love. I'm sorry I didn't come to you on Wednesday."

She nods, her hair tickling my chin as she tucks in below it. Cold feet slipping between my legs like they have for the past two decades.

"Any news from Clay?"

"Mercer said he looked okay when he left. He's better than he was last fall."

"Good." She sighs, sinking deeper. "He's lucky they didn't charge him with anything."

"I think we're lucky they mandated therapy. I don't know how dark it got for him, but I do know that not sleeping was only exacerbating the PTSD."

"Mmm," she hums in agreement.

"How's Addy been?"

While he's taken on more work at the ranch, we're still careful with what he's allowed to do. Leland's boy Hawken being here for a couple weeks this summer has been both a blessing and a curse. I thought Toby and Adler could get up to some shady shit, but the three of them are a wild time, for sure.

"He's missing his friend now that he's gone. He won't say it, but he's mad at me too. He told me he wanted to send Leni some money, to help her out. When I told him the trust mom left him is locked until he's eighteen, he accused me of gate-keeping it because I'm mad at Leni."

I couldn't stop the huff of laughter if I tried. Adler might be closest to Toby, but Leni is everyone's favorite sibling. Even if the older boys are annoyed and acting like assholes towards her. I know, without a doubt, if I asked them, they'd tell me that Leni was their favorite. Not a single one would be mad about it either, except, maybe Adler.

"I still can't believe she left everything to him."

Marcy sighs. "She gave me enough growing up, I didn't need her money. I'm just glad the other kids didn't get upset."

"To be fair, I don't think they realize just how much she left him."

"No, I suppose they don't."

"I thought for sure she was going to split it between the six of them."

"So did I, she changed her will after the trial though. She took him one day, so Leni and I could have a spa day together. Said she'd never met a braver boy."

"Brave to the point of recklessness." I sigh. "Had to drag him and Hawken out of the colt pen earlier today. They tried to bribe Destin into letting them get on a couple."

"Of course they did."

"They weren't completely unsuccessful either, Toby was putting his foot in the stirrup when I got there."

Marcy's eyes flash. Ire and something protective stirring up in her eyes.

"Destin handed him the reins of one that had just finished. He was done bucking, but the boys weren't taking no for an answer. Toby just happened to be the one closest. I think he fell in love with that horse, the way he was riding her around like they'd been doing it for years."

"Oh no." She gives me a knowing grin. "You lost another one then?"

"Yup, can't go selling that one now. Not gonna break my kid's heart."

"Which one is it?"

"The little bay mare. She's got some growin' to do, but I reckon he's going to out grow her when he hits high school. Might make a good trail horse for your retreat goers though. Once he moves on from her."

"Toby? Move on from something? No, I don't think so."

She's right. Toby still has every single belt he's ever worn. Every pair of boots that were his and not hand me downs. The kid is as sentimental as they come. Makes me love him a little more for it.

"Will you help me?" Marcy peeks up at me, her eyes half hidden by her lashes, the corner of her bottom lip stuck between her teeth. "Help me figure out how to get Leni back."

"Mar-"

"Not back home, just, I can't lose her. Not for good. I need your help."

"I'll help you. Whatever it takes, we'll get her back. Okay?"

"Okay."

Chapter 8

Wouldn't Change A Damn Thing

Marcy 55

"Marce? Where are—there you are." Orson appears in the doorway to Clay's old bedroom. "Hey pretty lady." He stoops down, one big hand on the small of my back, bringing me up into him for a kiss.

"Hello Mr. Kane." I can't stop the smile from taking over my face. "How was your day?"

"Better now." His smile is soft, tender even.

I hum into him, pecking one last kiss to his lips before I turn back to the task at hand. Clayton is coming home, finally. He stayed away longer than I anticipated, fourteen years wasn't on my bingo card. I wasn't thrilled when the boys got Mercer elected as Sheriff, but the moment that deputy position opened up, he convinced Clay it was time to come home.

"When does he get in?" Orson grabs the bottom of the full mattress, holding it up so I can fit the sheets around the corners.

"He graduates from the police academy on Friday, should be coming home with us on Saturday."

"Brooks making the trip?"

I stop my bustling to look at Orson. "He better fucking make the trip."

The only child I'll excuse is Eleanor. She hasn't seen or spoken to Clay in ten years. The boys had better all be there though. Mercer and Ethan were the only ones who made Clay's graduation from boot camp. This is our chance to show our support for him, to show him that he is still very much loved and wanted by this family.

"I'll talk to him and Destin. Shouldn't be a problem, not for the ranch at least."

I know he means Brooks. I couldn't tell you the last time he actually left the ranch and it wasn't work related. He's buried himself so deep into the job, I'm worried he forgot that there was more to life.

"What are we going to do with him? We should have pushed him to go to college, or take a vacation, something."

"You not enjoying my retirement?"

I scoff, giving him a little shove. Truth is, I am very much enjoying Orson doing less on the ranch. He still helps out, still has his hands in plenty, but all the little details are sorted by Brooks now. Orson can come home and take a nap, he can take his horse out just to ride, or spend his mornings sipping coffee with me. I don't mind that one bit.

What I do mind, is my eldest thinking that life is solely for working.

"You know damn well that's not what I meant."

"Fine." He pouts, slipping his hand in mine so he can walk me to our room. "How was this last retreat? It seemed like you had a good group."

"This group was fun." I beam up at him. "They called themselves corporate baddies."

"Baddies?" Orson shoots an eyebrow up, working the buttons of his shirt.

"It was all women, and honestly, so much more fun that way."

"City folks." He sighs. "Always giving men a bad name."

I have to laugh. "They're not all bad, but these women, they wanted the full experience. I haven't seen a group work so hard in a while. There was one gal, pretty thing too, she dug deep. I think she might have actually connected with some past life, because the girl knew how to swing a rope, and ride a horse. I was impressed."

"Damn, she need a job? We could always use another hand."

"Considering she's up for partner at her firm, I doubt she'll be coming back."

"Our loss then."

I follow him into the bathroom, watching him in the mirror as we brush our teeth.

"Anything on the Leni front?" He asks.

"No, as far as I know she has no plans for returning this summer. I didn't think she would, with Clay being home. She's going to have to visit eventually, but ripping that bandaid off will be hard."

"I still don't understand." Orson drops his toothbrush into the cup on the sink, turning to rest his hip on the counter. "What happened to those two? Wasn't there a bet about them getting together?"

"Oh God, the bets." A laugh bursts out of me, so many bets throughout the years. "They started a new one, betting how long it'll take for them to get together now that Clay's coming home."

Orson shakes his head, a smile creeping over his face. "Toby and Adler have a new one this summer too, the first one to get injured on a bronc gets two hundred dollars."

"Two hundred? What happened to betting chores and cheerios?"

He shrugs, wrapping an arm around my shoulder to lead me back into the bedroom, tucking me in before he turns on the side table lamp and switches off the big light.

"They've gotten too big for my pockets, that's for sure. I'm not betting more than a twenty here or there."

"Cheapskate," I tease, poking his arm before I turn to look at him. At fifty-six, Orson is all gray hair now. Wrinkles mar his tanned skin, the signs of age finally starting to really show. I cup his cheek, rubbing my thumb along the facial hair there. "When did we go and get old?"

He chuckles, turning his face in so he can kiss the heel of my palm. "Slowly but surely."

I sigh, a deep heavy sound that has him cocking his head.

"What's on your mind, Love?"

"Sometimes, I wish we could go back, do things different. Change things just a little, just enough that life was made a little easier."

"We have a pretty great life. One I'm proud of. I know we've had some bumps, some rocky times. But if changing those things means I don't have this." His gaze sweeps down my body, love and adoration in his eyes. "Then I wouldn't change a damn thing."

"No wonder the younger boys are such smooth talkers." I shake my head at him. A blush working its way up to my cheeks. Thirty-seven years and I still feel like a high school girl when he starts sweet talking me.

"I think Mercer fell in love with someone." He changes the subject, practically giving me whip lash.

"I'm sorry, what?"

"He's been all googly eyed at his phone. Always walking away when he takes phone calls. He's been unusually chill lately too, less dramatic, more philosophical."

"You think he met someone online?"

"Maybe? Hard to say, I haven't seen anyone around with him, nothing in the rumor mill either, but it does seem like he's got someone."

"Huh." I think back to my last few interactions with Mercer. I had noticed him staring off into space the other day, a dreamy look on his face. I hadn't even thought about the prospect of him with someone. He's another of my kids that works too hard. I don't think the boys realized how busy Mercer would be as sheriff, their plan backfiring a bit with how little we see him now.

"Well." I sigh. "At least if he is seeing someone, it's just one person. Mercer isn't the kind of guy to sleep around."

"And...who is?" Orson raises an eyebrow.

"Ethan, he's a manwhore."

Orson rears back, a laugh barking out of him before he's able to stop it. "We do not slut shame in this house, I believe you've said that more than once."

"I was defending my romance novels!" I shake my head, laughter bubbling up from my chest. "Fine, but Marlys asked me at Bridge the other day if he was interested in older women because she's seen him take four different women home from the bar in the last week and I can't un-hear it."

"Eesh, four in a week? Is he actually taking them home?"

"I don't know, nor do I want to. He needs a girl, someone to actually come home to."

"I don't disagree." He leans back against the headboard, his eyes closing. "We had six kids by his age, I can't quite wrap my head around their unwillingness to settle down. Marrying you was the best thing I ever did."

"It's a generational thing. They're busy building their lives first."

He pulls a face at me. "That's the best part, having someone to share it with. They're missing out."

"Give it some time," I chuckle. "Want to make a bet?"

That gets his attention, his head turning towards me slowly. "What kind of bet?"

"I bet you Leni and Clay will find their way back to each other by the end of the year."

"Hmm." He strokes his chin, pretending to think it over. "I give them a year. If Leni doesn't come back at all this summer, your bet is screwed."

"We'll see."

"What are the stakes though?"

"Twenty dollars?" I joke, a giggle slipping out before I can stop it.

"Twenty dollars?" He shakes his head, sliding closer in the bed. "Nah, I want a getaway. You win, we go to Hawaii. I win, we find a cabin in the woods to stay locked away for the week."

"I heartily accept your terms, Mr. Kane."

"Good." He leans down, taking my mouth in a slow kiss. The kind that has me panting by the time he pulls away. "Still kind of hot for me, aren't you Marcy Jo?"

"God yes," I breathe out, smoothing down my hair like we just got caught making out in his old Chevy pickup.

"So what'll it be tonight, Love?" He looks longingly at the kindle on his night stand. He's been enjoying the *read while you listen function*, some boring police procedural waiting for him to pick it back up.

I look over at my own kindle, the spicy enemies to lovers book waiting for me. We've taken to sharing our reading time, sometimes we listen to his, sometimes we listen to mine. Sometimes we sit next to each other and read in companionable silence, and sometimes, I manage to convince him to try something new.

"Rock paper scissors?" I offer my hands out in front of me.

"Rock, paper, scissors, shoot." He chants, his scissors falling victim to my closed fist. "Best two out of three," he begs.

Six more rounds and he finally concedes. He hasn't seemed to pick up on the fact that he uses the same pattern, every single time. Always scissors, then rock, then paper. It's incredibly easy to win when I want something done my way.

"Fine, what'll it be tonight?" He turns to me fully now, his kindle and headphones all but forgotten.

I scramble off the bed and find the book I finished yesterday, my favorite scene highlighted and tabbed so I could find it easier.

"Let's try this," I grin up at him, handing him the book, opened to the highlighted passage.

Orson turns back for his reading glasses, pushing them onto his face before he starts to read the book. The longer it takes for him to read the scene, the darker his face goes. Red taking over every single open patch of skin.

"Mar-" he clears his throat, his voice cracking. "We're too old for this, remember what happened last time you wanted to try out a scene from one of your books? I couldn't stand up straight for a week."

I grin, that had been exciting. Minus the pinched nerve in his back, I did feel bad about that. Everything before that had been very worth it—in my opinion.

"I'll break you in half!" he groans, tossing the book to the foot of the bed.

"I've been doing yoga with Iva. I swear I'm good. Please?" I pout my bottom lip at him, making my eyes wide and doe like.

"Fucking hell." He shakes his head, pulling me into his lap

before crashing his mouth into mine. "You drive me crazy, you know that?"

"I do," I squeal when he rubs his beard all over my bare skin. Tickling me, driving me crazy.

"How old are the characters in that book?"

"Um..." I have to think back. They weren't in their twenties, but they certainly weren't our age either. "Thirty-ish, maybe?"

Orson buries his face in my neck, a laugh making his shoulders shake.

"Alright, Mrs. Kane. You want me to bend you up into a pretzel, who am I to tell you no?"

"Now we're talking." I scramble off his lap, pulling my nightgown up over my head.

His pupils dilate, eyes taking in every inch of me.

"Best thing I've ever fucking done," he whispers, hands reaching as he pulls me back into him.

Best. Fucking. Thing.

Acknowledgments

This is my first time doing one of these, and there are honestly just too many people to thank when it comes to bringing these stories to life. I'll start with my husband, the one who's pushed me to pursue this dream. The one who has backed me every single step of the way. Thank you for believing in me, thank you for being my best friend and encouraging me to do the hard things. Thank you to my Tato. I wouldn't be the woman I am if I wasn't blessed by being your mama.

Thank you to all the people who came out and loved our family when we lost our Ryatt. Your support and community kept us here. It kept me here.

Thank you to Carolyn. I was this close to giving up on this dream when you reread DLMB and told me to be proud of it. Thank you for loving this one too. Thank you to Calli who has pumped me up from the very beginning. This series is as much for you now, as it is for me. I can't wait to serve you up Toby's book. Sorry about the weird American sayings.

To my sisters who have been my sounding board. Specifically my baby sis, sorry for traumatizing you. Thank you to my best friends who have been behind me every single step of the way. Cheering me on, sharing my posts, and waiting for these books.

Megan, I don't even know how to thank you for these gorgeous covers. I still can't wrap my brain around the fact that

I gave you terrible ideas and somehow you gave me these. Forever grateful for you!

About the Author

Bailey Johnson is a contemporary romance author who loves all things coffee and baked goods. She lives in rural North Dakota with her husband, son, obese dog, three cats and an ever growing flock of chickens.

If she's not writing you can usually find her exploring the farm with her son or out riding a borrowed horse. She's obsessed with all things cowboy and is really enjoying returning to her ranching roots. Even if it is only in fiction.

Find out more about Kane Ridge Ranch on her website
www.authorbaileyjohnson.com

Also by Bailey Johnson

Kane Ridge Ranch Series

Don't Leave Me Behind

Willow Park Novella Series

Make You Mine

Coming Soon

DON'T FORGET ABOUT ME

KANE RIDE RANCH BOOK 2

She's never had a family.

He thought he'd never need one.

Brooks Kane wants two things: to continue his Pa's legacy by running Kane Ridge Ranch, and some goddamn peace and quiet. But when his ex shows up and leaves him with a baby girl he never knew existed, Brooks' quiet life is thrown into chaos.

Desperate and in over his head, he hires a live-in nanny.

Pepper Basil has nothing tying her down and nowhere else to go. She's not exactly qualified to care for a child, but she can't afford to say no to the grumpy cowboy offering her a job and a place to stay.

She never expected to want a family that was never meant to be hers. He should have known that hiring sunshine in human form would be far too tempting for his own good...

But somewhere between late nights, shared responsibilities and a baby who needs them both, lines begin to blur.

Building a family was never part of the plan...but sometimes, the best family, isn't the one you're given, but the one you choose.

Pre-Order Don't Forget About Me Here

An Excerpt From
Don't Leave Me Behind

Chapter One Leni Fucking Kane

Clay

There's someone outside the cabin.

I swear I heard a car door thud. It was quiet, muffled, like someone parked far enough away that I'd be less likely to hear it. This feels like the beginning of a bad joke. I swear to God, if Adler is out there sneaking up on the cabin, I'm going to kill him. Slipping out of bed, I pad to the top of the stairs, squinting through the floor-to-ceiling windows at the front of Leni's cabin. The moon is high and bright, painting the landscape outside, but I still can't see anything that looks out of place.

Picking my way down the metal and wood staircase, I tiptoe over to the entry. It's possible that someone stopped along the highway and got out to take a piss, but I'm far enough from the road that I doubt I'd hear that. No, someone's on Kane land, real close to Leni's cabin. If they're here, expecting to find her asleep in her bed, they're in for a surprise.

A steady cadence of thuds indicates footsteps on the deck. I scan the living room for a weapon, remembering at the last second that I cleaned my rifle when I got home from work tonight. Adrenaline floods my veins as I tiptoe into the kitchen, where my duty rifle leans against a white wooden chair. Moonlight glimmers off the freshly oiled barrel. The magazine sits on the kitchenette table next to it. Five rounds, that's as far as I got before I squirreled my attention away to dinner and left it for tomorrow. I grab the gun and feed the magazine into its slot, hoping whoever is outside doesn't hear the click as it snaps into place.

My fingers pull back the charging handle as a key slides into the lock. *Who the fuck has a key?* No one in the family would sneak in here, not in the middle of the night. They know it would be a bad idea.

So, who is messing with me tonight?

Keeping the rifle ready in my hands, I wait, trying to hear over the sound of my heart banging against my chest. Anticipation coils deep in my gut. There's a pause once the door opens, the moonlight illuminating a silhouette that doesn't look like any of the Kane boys or the ranch hands. I'm about to demand they identify themselves when there's a crash, and the intruder goes flying to the ground.

I shoulder the rifle, ready to defend myself, before flicking on the lights. It only takes a couple of blinks before I can clearly see what's in front of me, and I think my heart stops beating for a second, because here she is.

The girl I've been avoiding since I was twenty-one, only, this is not the eighteen-year-old girl I saw last...*holy shit.* She is breathtakingly beautiful. Air rips from my lungs as I take her in. Long brown hair fans out around her head, wispy bangs hanging on either side of her face. Those big green eyes looking up at me with confusion, her movements slow and apprehensive. The terror in those eyes takes me back ten years. I swore to myself I'd never give her a reason to look at me like that again, but here we are. Her hands are trembling in surrender while I'm pointing a gun at her, in her own cabin. Why...why is she sneaking into the cabin when she's supposed to know I'm here?

"What. The. Fuck?" she snarls.

I move the barrel of the rifle away, aiming at the floor. A sound somewhere between a groan and a growl escapes her as she struggles to stand. *Did I shoot her and not remember? Was she hurt somehow?* I take inventory when she's standing in front of me, checking for injury. Her hoodie hangs loosely on her, the sleeves bunching at her wrists, too long for her short arms. Black leggings hug every single curve and dip of her legs, drawing my eyes straight down to the bright pink running shoes on her feet.

There's no blood or wounds that I can see, and while I want to sigh in relief, I'm too aware of how close I came to shooting her. I can't believe I aimed a gun at Leni. Mercer's little sister, baby girl of the entire Kane family.

My Leni.

I could have shot her.

With that thought, I drop the rifle, stumbling back. Leni tilts her head, her lips moving, but I can't hear anything other than the word *shot,* ricocheting through my brain like a fucking pinball. I'm no longer in the cabin. Even though I can see her, her words don't reach me. Instead, my heart hammers out a steady beat to a volley of gunshots and mortar rounds, to shouts of 'Grenade!' and 'Medic!' I glance down at my hands; they're red, covered in the blood of a fallen Marine, and I can't breathe.

My chest tightens, black creeping at the edges of my vision, every inhale a struggle. It's been years since I've had an attack this bad. I've gone through extensive therapy, done the hard work to get myself out of the dark, and back into something resembling a real, living human again. This isn't supposed to be happening, especially not in front of Leni.

I claw at my shirt, desperate to rip the fabric off, as if that might help me breathe. I watch from a distance, detached, while Leni kneels in front of me. She touches my face, and my hands itch to defend myself from a threat that isn't real. I will not hurt her, no matter how fucked up my brain is right now.

I will not hurt Leni. Not again.

Her lips are moving, but I still can't hear anything past the sounds of gunfire and explosions. I flinch as a mortar round lands too close to us.

Clay. Her lips make the shape of my name, repeatedly, but I can't break through, can't claw my way to the surface to reach her. I want to yell at her to go, will myself to fucking pass out, and be done with this whole thing. I don't want to see her look at me with pity and concern, or worse, fear. She's looked at me with fear in her eyes before. I thought it would destroy me; part of me died *that* day.

I should've known Eleanor Kane doesn't scare easily. She proved that ten years ago, showing up on my doorstep, willing to lose herself to fix me. I should've expected that same look of sheer determination now, as her eyes dart around, searching for a solution. I feel as lost as she looks; none of my usual panic attack exercises come to mind. Maybe the lack of sleep is catching up to me. I should've taken the damn sleeping pills Doc prescribed. This is *exactly* what I want to avoid.

Clay. Those pretty, pink lips, mouth once more. Something like hesitation sparks to life in her deep green eyes. I try to look away, shame gnawing at me, my lungs tightening. She doesn't let me. Soft fingers guide my face back to hers as she leans forward and crashes her lips against mine.

The moment her lips touch mine, it's like someone hit pause, and I remember how to breathe again.

There's no more gunshots, no more screaming; only ragged breathing and jittery hands as the adrenaline seeps out of my body. I reach for her, needing something solid, something real to hold onto, careful not to grip too tight. I'm desperate to make sure she's actually there, kissing me. Her scent of lilacs and vanilla wafts from her undone hair into my nose. A scent so familiar and nostalgic that my chest starts to hurt for a different reason.

Wrapping my arms around her, I haul her into me, crushing her body against my chest, kissing her back. She tenses, muscles locking up beneath my hands. Pain slices through my lip as she sinks her teeth in. It's not a love bite, but a warning. I jerk back, slamming my head into the wall as she scrambles off me. Her chest rises and falls with each ragged breath she takes. Her hands shake, and when she manages to open her eyes to look at me, I gasp. She's angry. Livid. I think I could count on one hand the amount of times I've seen Leni this angry.

The taste of iron fills my mouth, the sting barely enough to rein me in. Leni Kane was in my lap, kissing me. I'm really fucking trying to remind myself why I can't go there with her, but it's so damn hard. Breathing the same air, staring at that gorgeous face. I realize how badly I still want her, even with that scowl.

"What the fuck are you doing in my cabin, Clay?"

I barely suppress the shudder that threatens to overtake me when she says my name. It's been too long since I've seen her. Too long since I've heard her voice, even if my name is dripping with venom when she says it. After a decade of doing my best to avoid her, I deserve that.

"Your parents have those corporate retreat things going on, and I felt like I was getting in the way. Mercer told me he asked you. He said you weren't coming back for the summer, so I've been staying here the past couple of months."

"Oh." Her eyes dart toward the door, then back to me. Fear and uncertainty fill them. That fear shouldn't be there, and knowing I caused it makes me sick to my stomach.

"I thought you knew." Scrubbing both hands down my face, I try to rein in the emotions I have flooding in and out of my system. "I, uh, I'll head over to Merc's. Come back for my stuff in the morning."

"No!" she says.

I crook an eyebrow at her, wondering, for the first time, what the hell she's doing here in the middle of the night.

"No, sorry...*fuck*." She draws her knees up into her chest, pulling her sleeves down and around her thumbs the way she used to when she was younger. "I don't want them to know I'm here."

"They're gonna know you're here, Len. That's why your dad wanted you in this cabin, so they can keep an eye on you."

"No, I know. I'm not an amateur." She rolls her eyes, huffing in frustration. *Fuck she's cute.* "I've done it before. I park in the trees, keep the lights off after dark. I just...I need a few days to regroup before they get all up in my business again."

I highly doubt they don't know when she's here. It's more believable that they realize when she sneaks back home and figures she wants to be left alone.

My fingers itch with the desire to pull her back into me. To feel the weight of her in my arms. I'd do anything if she'd let me kiss her again, just one more time. It'll never be enough where Leni is concerned, but it would be something. The longer I hesitate, the more restless she becomes, crossing and uncrossing her arms, straightening her legs only to pull them back to her chest. Something's wrong. Something happened, and I want to fix it. Not that I have any right or that I should even be looking at her like this, but I still want to fix it. Leni in pain will never do.

Ever.

"Right, I—uh. I'll crash out on the couch until morning and go get a room from the Inn. No big deal."

She looks aghast, like I told some salacious bit of gossip. "You can't go to the inn! Then everyone will know."

"Know what, Leni?"

"Why would you leave here to stay at the inn?"

"I don't know, because you..." *Oh.* She rolls her eyes at me again, and I can't lie, the sass she's giving me is doing nothing to help the situation that has arisen in my pants. I mean, she was just sitting on me, kissing me. It's not entirely my fault.

Okay, fuck, it is my fault, and I feel like a fucking creep right now. Drawing one of my legs up, I try to hide the fact that I am sporting a semi-hard dick.

It's not solely the kiss; it's everything about her. Freckles dust her nose, which still crinkles when she's annoyed. Her hair's shorter than I remember, but it looks good. Natural waves hit right below her shoulders. I want to reach forward, run my hands through it again, wrap it around my fist while I—you know what? Nope. *Down boy.* You are not going there. Not with Leni *fucking* Kane.

The realization of what she hasn't said hits me like a bucket of ice-cold water. Does she really think we can stay here together? "You want me to stay here with you?"

She's been back in my life for all of five minutes, and I've already had my tongue in her mouth. I have zero control when it comes to this girl. I've worked my ass off to stay away from her, so I wouldn't have to deal with this.

Eleanor is all sunshine and goodness, and she deserves someone who can reflect that back. Not someone dark and twisted like me. I won't saddle her with my mess when she has her whole life ahead of her.

"Yeah, Clay, that's the idea."

"No," I snap, the words coming out harsher than I mean. Pushing off the floor, I stomp up the stairs. I need to get my shit and get out of here before I do something even more stupid.

Something I can't take back.

www.ingramcontent.com/pod-product-compliance
Lightning Source LLC
LaVergne TN
LVHW051016080826
845145LV00009B/2654